This book belongs to:

_____

For Anna, for all your help and support from beginning to end. And for Amelia and George, my bug collectors.

This paperback edition was published for Scottish Book Trust in 2021 by Andersen Press Ltd.

First published in Great Britain in 2019 by Andersen Press Ltd.,

20 Vauxhall Bridge Road, London, SW1V 2SA, UK.

Vijverlaan 48, 3062 HL Rotterdam, Nederland.

Copyright © Alex G Griffiths, 2019.

The right of Alex G Griffiths to be identified as the

author and illustrator of this work has been

asserted by him in accordance with the

Copyright, Designs and Patents Act, 1988.

All rights reserved.

Printed and bound in India.

1 3 5 7 9 10 8 6 4 2

British Library Cataloguing in Publication Data available.

The Bug Collector

Alex G Griffiths

ANDERSEN PRESS

Today was George's favourite
day of the whole week.
It was Sunday, and that
meant that he was going on
an adventure with Grandad.

This particular Sunday Grandad took George to...

... the Museum of Wildlife!
Inside, they saw ferocious dinosaurs,

wondrous whales,

massive mammoths and
even stranger creatures of
every colour and shape.

INSECT WORLD →

Chop chop, Georgie!

SO COOL!

But Grandad didn't stop to look at any of it.
He was too excited about something completely different...

The creatures he wanted to show George were
much smaller and stranger, and Grandad loved them.

On the journey home, George
could think of nothing else but the
marvellous bugs he had seen that day.

That night, George's dreams were filled with buzzing
bees, floating butterflies and sliding snails.

When he woke up, George couldn't wait to get outside.

SO EXCITED!

He packed his rucksack and headed
out to see what he could find.

In the garden, he noticed bugs everywhere!

Something fluttered
past George's face.

He tried to catch it...

... but it was too quick for him!

Catching bugs was not as easy as George had thought.

They were so clever. They always seemed to know what he was going to do.

George had to learn to be even more
cunning to outwit them.

Soon, he was a master bug catcher!

With his rucksack and cart full up,
George set off for his tree house.

After he'd found a place
for every bottle and jar,
George admired his collection.

Examining them closely, he saw so many
different shapes and colours.

As George went home for dinner,
everything seemed silent and still.

Nothing

buzzed,

fluttered

or scuttled.

IT'S SO QUIET...

The next day, he went back
to the garden to continue the hunt.

But everywhere was dull and sad.

Grandad was also wondering what was going on.

OOPS!

He knew something didn't seem right.

Suddenly Grandad realised: all the bugs had gone!

Back at the tree house, George looked at his collection. The bugs didn't look happy.

Grandad wasn't happy either when he
saw what George had been doing.

He loved bugs as much as George, but knew that
living ones shouldn't be kept in jars and bottles.

Grandad explained to George the important jobs
bugs have in the outside world, especially in our gardens.

Bees help to make lots of new
flowers by carrying **pollen**
from one to another.

Ladybirds also help plants
by eating up to **five hundred**
aphids a day!

Ants are natural farmers, carrying seeds and planting them in new places.

Dung beetles turn waste into food!

And of course, all insects are an important part of the natural food chain. If we take them away lots of animals won't get their dinner.

George listened carefully. He knew what he had to do.

He opened the jars,
the bottles, the windows
and doors, and the
bugs flew out.

The sky was alive again!

George was sad to see them go.

But Grandad was smiling. He had an idea…

It took a little while, but together, they changed the garden into a bug sanctuary to share with everyone.

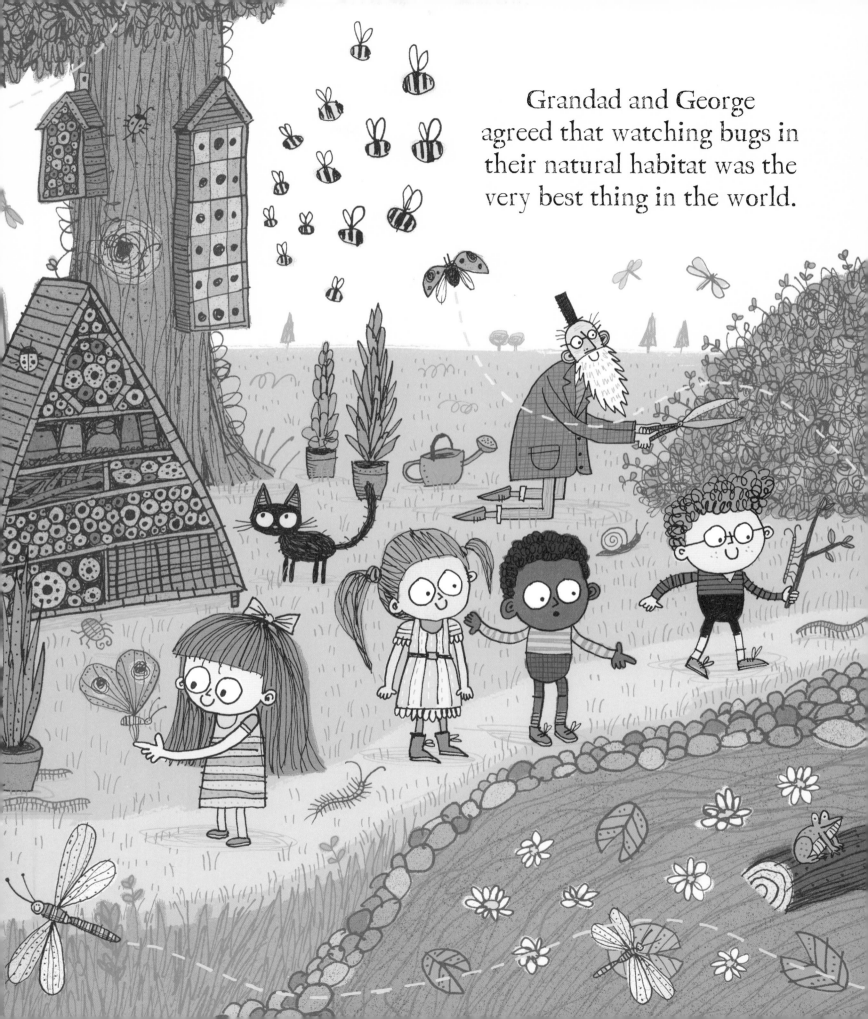

Grandad and George agreed that watching bugs in their natural habitat was the very best thing in the world.